FABER CLASS[...]

The It-Doesn't-Matter Suit

and Other Stories

FABER & FABER

has published children's books since 1929. Some of our very first publications included *Old Possum's Book of Practical Cats* by T. S. Eliot, starring the now world-famous Macavity, and *The Iron Man* by Ted Hughes. Our catalogue at the time said that 'it is by reading such books that children learn the difference between the shoddy and the genuine'. We still believe in the power of reading to transform children's lives.

→ FABER CLASSICS ←

The It-Doesn't-Matter Suit

and other stories

SYLVIA PLATH

with illustrations by David Roberts

ff

FABER & FABER

This collection first published in 2001 by Faber & Faber Limited
Bloomsbury House, 74–77 Great Russell Street
London WC1B 3DA
This edition first published in 2014
The Bed Book was first published in 1976
The It-Doesn't-Matter Suit was first published in 1996
Mrs Cherry's Kitchen was first published in 2001

Designed and typeset by Crow Books

Printed and bound in Great Britain by CPI Group (UK), Croydon CR0 4YY

A CIP record for this book is available from the British Library

ISBN 978–0–571–31464–5

2 4 6 8 10 9 7 5 3

Contents

The It-Doesn't-Matter Suit

Max Nix was seven years old, and the youngest of seven brothers. First came Paul, the eldest and tallest of all seven. Then came Emil. Then Otto and Walter, and Hugo and Johann.

Last came Max. Max's whole name was Maximilian, but because he was only seven he did not need such a big name. So everybody called him just Max. Max lived with Mama and Papa Nix and his six brothers in a little village called Winkelburg, halfway up a steep mountain.

The mountain had three peaks, and on all three peaks, winter and summer, sat caps of snow like three big scoops of vanilla ice-cream. On nights when the moon rose round and bright as an orange balloon you could hear the foxes barking in the dark pine forest high above Max's house. On clear, sunlit days you could see the river winking and blinking far, far below in the valley, small and thin as a silver ribbon.

Max liked where he lived.

Max was happy, except for one thing.

More than anything else in the world Max Nix wanted a suit of his own.

He had a green sweater and green wool socks and a green felt hunting hat with a turkey feather in it. He even had a fine pair of leather knickers with carved bone buttons. But everybody knows a sweater and a pair of knickers are not the same thing as a suit – a made-to-order suit with long trousers and a jacket to match.

Wherever Max Nix looked in Winkelburg – east and west, north and south, high and low and round about – he saw people wearing suits. Some people had suits for work, and these were very sturdy suits of brown or grey cloth. Some people had suits for weddings, and these were very handsome suits with striped silk waistcoats. Some people had suits for skiing, and these were gay blue or red suits with rows of snowflakes or edelweiss embroidered on the cuffs and collars.

Some people had summer suits of linen, white and crisp as letter paper. Papa Nix and Paul and Emil and Otto and Walter and Hugo and Johann all had suits. *Everybody* on the mountain had some sort of suit except Max.

Now Max did not want a suit *just* for work

(that would be too plain)

or *just* for weddings

(that would be too fancy)

or *just* for skiing

(that would be too hot)

or *just* for summer

(that would be too cool).

He wanted a suit for All-Year-Round.

He wanted a suit for doing Everything. Not too plain a suit for birthdays and holidays, and not too fancy a suit for school and calling the cows home. Not too hot a suit for hiking in July, and not too cool a suit for coasting in the snow.

If Max had a suit for All-Year-Round, the butcher and the baker, and the blacksmith and the goldsmith, and the tinker and the tailor, and the innkeeper, and the schoolteacher, and the grocer and the goodwives, and the minister and the mayor, and everybody else in Winkelburg would flock to their doors and windows when he went by. 'Look!' they would murmur to one another. 'There goes Maximilian in his marvellous suit!'

If Max had
a suit for doing
Everything, the
cats in the alleys
and the dogs on the
cobbles of Winkelburg
would follow him uptown and
downtown, purring and grrring
with admiration.

That was the sort of suit Max was dreaming about the day the postman of Winkelburg knocked on the Nixes' door and delivered the big package.

The package was shaped like a long, flattish box.

It was wrapped round with heavy brown wrapping paper.

It was tied with red string.

Across the top of the package Max spelled out N-I-X in large black letters. The first name had been rained on and not even the Postmaster of Winkelburg could read it. So nobody knew *which* Nix the package was for.

The package might be for Papa Nix, or Paul or Emil, or Otto or Walter, or Hugh or Johann. It might even be for Max. Nobody could tell for sure.

Mama Nix had just baked a batch of apricot tarts. Everybody sat around the kitchen table, wondering who the package was for, and who it was from, and what was in it, eating up the apricot tarts one by one.

It was not Christmastime, so it was not a Christmas present.

It was not near anybody's birthday, so it was not a birthday present.

'It is too short,' said Paul, 'to be a pair of skis.'

'It is too small,' said Emil, 'to be a toboggan.'

'It is too light,' said Otto, lifting the package easily, 'to be a bicycle.'

'It is too wide,' said Walter, 'to be a fishing rod.'

'It is too large,' said Hugo, 'to be a hunting knife.'

Johann put his ear to the package and gave it a little shake. 'It is too quiet,' he said, 'to be a cow bell.'

Max did not say anything. It is too fine, he thought to himself, to be for me.

At last the apricot tarts were all gone, and still nobody could guess what was in the package.

'Let us open it,' everybody said.

Papa Nix untied the knot in the red string.

Mama Nix unwrapped the brown paper. Inside the brown paper was a grey cardboard box. Paul lifted the lid off the box. Inside the grey box was a lot of white tissue paper. Emil and Otto and Walter and Hugo and Johann and Max all helped to pull away some of the tissue paper.

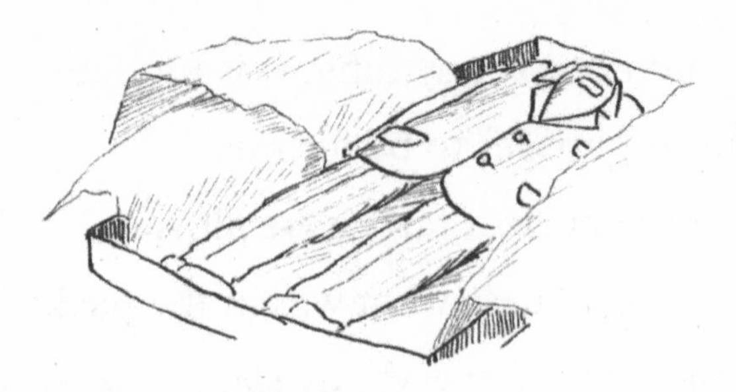

And there in the grey box with a wreath of white tissue paper around it lay a

woolly

whiskery

brand-new

mustard-yellow

suit

with three brass buttons shining like mirrors on the front of it, and two brass buttons at the back, and a brass button on each cuff.

'What a strange suit,' said Papa Nix. 'I have

never seen anything quite like it.'

'It is made of good strong cloth,' said Mama Nix, feeling the yellow wool between thumb and forefinger. '*This* suit will not wear out in a hurry.'

'It is a handsome suit!' said Paul.

'Light as a feather!' said Emil.

'Bright as butter!' said Otto.

'Warm as toast!' said Walter.

'Simply fine!' said Hugo.

'Dandy!' said Johann.

'O my!' said Max.

Every one of the seven brothers wished he owned just such a suit.

But the suit looked as if it might be Papa Nix's size. So Papa Nix tried it on. The jacket

was wide enough, and the trousers were long enough. The suit fitted Papa Nix to a T.

'I shall wear the suit to work tomorrow,' he said. Papa Nix worked in a bank. He thought how it would be to wear the woolly, whiskery, brand-new, mustard-yellow suit to work. Such a suit had never been seen before in all Winkelburg. What would the people say? Perhaps they would think the suit was too gay for a sensible banker. Those brass buttons would flash out like big coins. All the other bankers wore dark blue or dark grey suits. None of them ever wore a mustard-yellow suit.

At last Papa Nix sighed and said, 'I am too big to wear a mustard-yellow suit.'

Paul held his breath.

'I will give the suit to Paul,' said Papa Nix.

So Paul tried on the mustard-yellow suit. Paul was as tall as Papa Nix, so the trousers were the right length. He was not as broad as Papa Nix around the middle though, so the jacket hung about him in loose, flapping folds. But Mama Nix was clever with a needle and thread. She took a tuck here and a stitch there. When she was through, the suit fitted Paul to a T.

'I shall wear the suit skiing tomorrow,' he said.

Paul often went skiing with his friends.

He thought how it would be to wear the woolly, whiskery, brand-new, mustard-yellow suit skiing. Such a suit had never been seen before in all Winkelburg. What would his friends say? Perhaps they would think yellow was a silly colour for a ski-suit. He would look like a meadow of sunflowers against the snow. All his friends wore red ski-suits or blue ski-suits. None of them ever wore a mustard-yellow suit.

At last Paul sighed and said, 'I, also, am too big to wear a mustard-yellow suit.'

Emil held his breath.

'Let Emil try on the suit,' said Paul.

So Emil tried on the mustard-yellow suit. Emil was as broad as Paul, but shorter. The cuffs of the jacket covered his hands, and the cuffs of the trousers folded down over his shoes. But Mama Nix took a tuck here and a stitch there. When she was through the suit fitted Emil to a T.

'I shall wear the suit in the toboggan race tomorrow,' he said.

Emil was a member of the Winkelburg toboggan team. Once a month the Winkelburg team raced the team of the town on the other side of the mountain. He thought how it would be to wear the woolly, whiskery, brand-new, mustard-yellow suit in the toboggan races. Such a suit had never been seen before in all Winkelburg. What would his team-mates say? Perhaps they would think he was trying to show off in the mustard-yellow suit.

He would look like a streak of lightning going down the toboggan track. All his team-mates wore brown zipper-jackets and brown pants. None of them ever wore a mustard-yellow suit.

At last Emil sighed and said, 'I, also, am too big to wear a mustard-yellow suit.'

Otto held his breath.

'Maybe the suit will be right for Otto,' said Emil.

So Otto tried on the mustard-yellow suit. Otto was almost as tall as Emil, only his shoulders were not quite so broad. The jacket drooped a little. But Mama Nix took a tuck here and a stitch there.

When she was through the suit fitted Otto to a T.

'I shall wear the suit on my paper round tomorrow,' he said.

Otto delivered newspapers on his bicycle. He thought how it would be to wear the woolly, whiskery, brand-new, mustard-yellow suit on his paper round. Such a suit had never been seen before in all Winkelburg. What would his customers say? Perhaps they would think the suit was too fancy for a paperboy. He might

splash mud on it or be caught in the rain, and then what a sorry sight he would be. All the other paperboys wore their old clothes when they delivered papers.

None of them ever wore a brand-new, mustard-yellow suit.

At last Otto sighed and said, 'I, also, am too big to wear a mustard-yellow suit.'

Walter held his breath.

'If the suit fits me, it should fit Walter,' said Otto.

So Walter tried on the mustard-yellow suit. Walter was a little shorter than Otto, and a little thinner.

But Mama Nix took a tuck here and a stitch there and moved the brass buttons over an inch. When she was through the suit fitted Walter to a T.

'I shall wear the suit ice-fishing tomorrow,' he said.

Walter often went ice-fishing in Winkelburg Lake in the winter. He thought how it would be to wear the woolly, whiskery, brand-new, mustard-yellow suit ice-fishing. Such a suit had never been seen before in all Winkelburg. What would the fish think? Perhaps the suit would frighten them away. It would glow through the ice like a bright sun. The other fishermen all wore green suits in the summer so the fish could not tell them from leaves, and brown suits in the winter so the fish could not tell them from tree trunks. None of them ever wore a mustard-yellow suit.

At last Walter sighed and said, 'I, also, am too big to wear the mustard-yellow suit.'

Hugo held his breath.

'Perhaps Hugo might like to wear it,' said Walter.

So Hugo tried on the mustard-yellow suit. Hugo was a good deal shorter than Walter, but Mama Nix snipped a bit here and trimmed a bit there with her scissors and turned the thread-ends under. When she was through the suit fitted Hugo to a T.

'I shall wear the suit hunting tomorrow,' he said.

Hugo often went fox-hunting in the forest above Winkelburg, for the foxes stole the plump Winkelburg chickens. He thought how it would be to wear the woolly, whiskery, brand-new, mustard-yellow suit fox-hunting. Such a suit had never been seen before in all Winkelburg. What would the fox think? Perhaps the fox would just hide in a hole and laugh at him. The brass buttons would beam like lanterns from far off and warn the fox he was coming. All the other hunters wore checked and speckled suits so the fox could not see them easily in the checked and speckled shade of the forest. None of them ever wore a mustard-yellow suit.

At last Hugo sighed and said, 'I, also, am too big to wear a mustard-yellow suit.'

Johann held his breath.

'Let's see how the suit looks on Johann,' said Hugo.

So Johann tried on the mustard-yellow suit.

Johann was shorter and rounder than Hugo, but Mama Nix snipped here and clipped there and moved the buttons back to the edge of the jacket.

When she was through the suit fitted Johann to a T.

'I shall wear the suit for milking the cows tomorrow,' he said.

Johann took turns with his six brothers milking Papa Nix's cows. He thought how it would be to wear the woolly, whiskery, brand-new, mustard-yellow suit for milking the cows. Such a suit had never been seen before in all Winkelburg. What would the cows think?

Perhaps they would take him for a bundle of whiskery yellow hay and nibble at his collar. Everybody else wore blue overalls for milking cows. Nobody ever wore a mustard-yellow suit.

At last Johann sighed and said, 'Even I am too big to wear a mustard-yellow suit.' Max could hardly keep from jumping up and down, but he held still as a mouse and waited to see what would happen.

'Max has no suit,' said Johann.

'Goodness!' said Papa Nix.

'Gracious!' said Mama Nix.

'Let it be Max's suit,' everybody said, nodding and smiling.

So Max tried on the mustard-yellow suit. Max was the shortest and thinnest of all the Nix brothers, but Mama Nix snipped and stitched and took tucks and moved buttons.

When she was through the suit fitted Max as if it were made-to-order.

'I shall wear the suit,' Max said, 'today and tomorrow and the day after that.'

Max went to school in his mustard-yellow suit.

He walked straight and he sat tall, and pretty soon the schoolchildren began to wish they had suits like the suit Max wore. So even though nobody in Winkelburg had ever seen such a suit before

IT DIDN'T MATTER.

Max went skiing in his mustard-yellow suit. He slipped and slid for a way on the seat of his pants, but the cloth of the suit was very strong and didn't rip, so

IT DIDN'T MATTER.

Max rode his bicycle in his mustard-yellow suit.

He got caught in the rain, but the drops ran right off the whiskery suit like drops off a duck's back, so

IT DIDN'T MATTER.

Max went ice-fishing in his mustard-yellow suit.

The fish came swimming up to see what gleamed so bright on the other side of the ice, and Max caught enough for supper. He got some fish scales on his suit, but everybody was so busy admiring Max's fish that they never noticed, so

IT DIDN'T MATTER.

Max went coasting in his mustard-yellow suit. He tipped over once or twice and landed in a cold snowbank, but the woolly suit was very warm, so

IT DIDN'T MATTER.

Max went fox-hunting in his mustard-yellow suit. The fox saw something yellow through the trees and thought it was a fat, yellow Winkelburg chicken. His mouth started to water and he came running. Max caught the fox. He lost a brass button in the bushes, but the button shone out like a star in the dark forest and he found it again, so

IT DIDN'T MATTER.

Max milked the cows in his mustard-yellow suit. The suit's sunny colour made the cows dream of buttercups and daisies in the spring meadows, and they mooed for happiness. When Max finished the milking he had three pails full of the creamiest milk ever seen in Winkelburg. Some pieces of hay stuck to the suit, but the hay was yellow and the suit was yellow and the hay didn't show, so

IT DIDN'T MATTER.

Max walked uptown and downtown and round about Winkelburg in his mustard-yellow suit.

When he went by, the butcher and the baker, the blacksmith and the goldsmith, the tinker and the tailor, the innkeeper and the schoolteacher, the grocer and the goodwives, the minister and the mayor all leaned out of their doors and windows.

'Look!' they murmured to one another. 'There goes Maximilian in his marvellous suit.'

And the cats in the alleys and the dogs on the cobbles of Winkelburg followed at his heels, purring and grrring with admiration for Max Nix

and his

wonderful

woolly

whiskery

brand-new

mustard-yellow

IT-DOESN'T-MATTER SUIT.

Mrs Cherry's Kitchen

SPORT
DAILY NEWS

Mrs Myrtle May Cherry had the spickest, spannest, shiniest, merriest kitchen in all Appleton Lane. Everybody said so, and they say so still. From Mrs Cherry's kitchen floated the most delicious smells. Fried chicken and blue-berry cupcakes one day, crackling pork roast and gingerbread the next. No wonder Mr and Mrs Cherry grew round and rosy.

Now on one certain Monday morning, sun came streaming in through Mrs Cherry's kitchen windows and made a square of light, yellow as butter, on the sparkling linoleum floor. The smell of savoury bacon and hot coffee perfumed the air.

'Pong!' said Toaster, and up popped two slices of golden toast. One for Mrs Cherry and one for

Mr Cherry. Mrs Cherry put strawberry jam on her toast, and Mr Cherry spread clover-blossom honey on his.

'Mmm!' murmured Mr Cherry dreamily. 'I *do* enjoy crisp toast in the morning.'

'Thanks to our fine, shiny toaster,' Mrs Cherry said. 'It's made us golden-brown toast each day without fail all these years.' And at these words, Toaster fairly glistened with pride.

'Blrip. Blrip,' gurgled Coffee Percolator, not to be outdone, and winked on his red eye.

Mrs Cherry poured out steaming coffee in two blue-bordered cups. 'You know,' she smiled at her husband, 'this coffee percolator makes such uncommonly good coffee that I sometimes think it must be magic!'

Mrs Cherry didn't know how true her words were. Even as she spoke, the kitchen pixies poked each other and giggled behind the sugar tin. Now way back in Mrs Cherry's great-grandmother's day, there were special kitchen pixies to turn the churned milk into butter and to see that bread rose light and crusty in the old-fashioned ovens. Sometimes, when

these pixies felt mischievous, they'd curdle the cream or unsettle the laying hens. But mostly they were good, reliable pixies. And often, at night, wise housewives set out saucers of porridge on the doorstep for them, with honey and raisins in it.

Mrs Cherry had no idea that two descendants of these pixies lived right in her kitchen. These two pixies had long, unpronounceable names, handed down from father to son and from mother to daughter. But they called themselves Salt and Pepper for short. One pixie wore a white suit and slept in Mrs Cherry's silver salt-shaker, while the other pixie wore a speckled brown suit and slept in Mrs Cherry's silver pepper-shaker. It was their job to see that all the kitchen folk did their daily work and lived in harmony and content.

After Mr Cherry had found his tortoise-shell-rimmed spectacles which he claimed some imp hid away every morning just for fun, he kissed Mrs Cherry goodbye and left for work.

Mrs Cherry hummed to herself, sitting at the sunny kitchen table and paring carrots for Mr Cherry's favourite supper of beef stew. She flashed a bright, happy look around her kitchen: at the washing machine, and at the oven baking, and at the icebox rumbling gently as it kept the vanilla ice-cream cold for Mr Cherry's dessert.

'What a fortunate woman I am!' Mrs Cherry said aloud to no one in particular.

'Fortunate is right,' murmured Icebox.

'To be sure,' whispered Oven.

'Brumm,' Washing Machine cleared her throat. 'Exactly so.'

But Mrs Cherry couldn't understand their language, and so she didn't answer.

Now on this particular morning, the pixies received some complaints from the kitchen folk for the first time. Each one felt he could do his own work well enough, but each one of them cast longing looks at the jobs the other kitchen folk did.

'It's not that I don't *like* whipping eggs,' explained Egg-Beater. 'It's just that Iron turns out such frilly white ruffled blouses

for Mrs Cherry. I'm sure I could make lovely white ruffles on Mrs Cherry's blouses too, if I were given the chance. Just look how beautiful and frothy my whipped cream is! I'd like a change of chores for a day.'

'Ssss. So would I!' sighed Iron. 'I'd like to take over Cousin Waffle-Iron's work. Mr Cherry smacks his lips over those waffly waffles. But I could make even better dents with my shiny tip. Do let me try!'

Believe it or not, every electric appliance in Mrs Cherry's kitchen had a similar request! Washing Machine wanted to bake a sponge cake. Oven wanted to iron Mr Cherry's shirts

crisp as piecrusts.

Coffee Percolator longed to taste ice cream.

'I'm sure I could be cold as Icebox,' Coffee Percolator boasted, 'if I just put my mind to it.'

'And I,' bragged Toaster, 'could pop out bettershaped icecubes at the drop of a hat!'

All this while Mrs Cherry was merrily cutting up potatoes and onions to toss into Mr Cherry's stew without an inkling of the problem facing Salt and Pepper.

'If we don't satisfy the kitchen folk,' Salt whispered to Pepper, who was skating thoughtfully from cube to cube on the icecube tray, 'they may go on strike and stop work altogether. And then where would Mrs Cherry be!'

‘Do you suppose,’ Pepper said, ‘we should let them try it?’

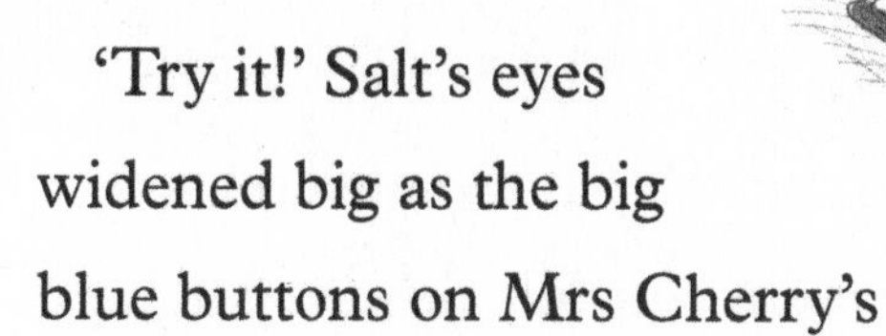

‘Try it!’ Salt’s eyes widened big as the big blue buttons on Mrs Cherry’s best dress. ‘Why, think of the mess they’d make!’

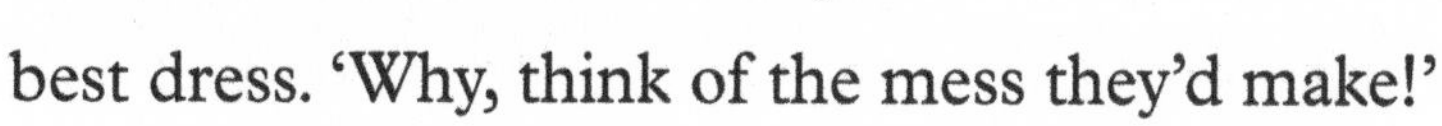

‘It *would* mean a lot of extra work for us, of course,’ Pepper admitted. ‘But it’s our job to keep the kitchen folk happy.’

Salt considered, chewing a leaf of parsley. ‘As Mr Cherry remarks so often,’ Salt said at last, ‘experience is the best teacher.’

Pepper nodded. ‘Once the kitchen folk *experience* how impossible it is to do each other's work, they'll be twice as happy tending to their own. But we mustn't let on that we doubt their talent.'

'No,' Salt agreed. 'Let them find out for themselves.'

So the pixies shook hands on their secret.

'Done!' And they went out to calm the kitchen folk.

'We say okay,' Pepper sang, 'to each one.'

'Choose your day,' sang Salt, 'and have fun.'

All the kitchen folk hummed and whirred and clicked with delight.

'Let's do it this very day!' Egg-Beater cried. And everybody joined in. 'Let's make today the day for Operation Change-About!'

They decided to wait for a moment when

Mrs Cherry's back was turned: when she was talking on the telephone, or visiting a neighbour's, and then! Icebox purred with dreams of cooking an honest-to-goodness plum tart instead of merely keeping the milk and butter cold. Iron glided sizzling over damp sheets, picturing acres of artistically dented waffles.

All the kitchen folk waited eagerly for Mrs Cherry to leave them alone. Just for five minutes! Then they could show her how versatile they were. But Mrs Cherry spent that whole Monday morning scouring and scurrying around the kitchen, whisking away invisible dust, polishing silver that gleamed to begin with, washing, mixing cake batter, ironing her best dirndl skirt with the daisies on it. She didn't turn her back for a minute. The kitchen folk hummed and whirred and sizzled in impatience. When would they have a chance for their wonderful Change-About?

But just before lunch-time, as they were all ready to give up their marvellous plan in despair, Sunny and Bunny, the Dimbleby twins, chorused from Mrs Cherry's back porch:

'Oh, Mrs Cherry! Come and see our new kittens! Fudge Ripple has *five* new kittens!'

Fudge Ripple was half Sunny's cat, and half Bunny's cat. She was mostly white, with long ripply black marks, and reminded the twins of their favourite ice cream.

'Whew!' breathed Icebox.

'Ah,' rejoiced Oven. 'Here we go now!'

Sure enough, Mrs Cherry was brushing the flour from her hands and untying her apron strings. Then she followed Sunny and Bunny down the back steps. Through the kitchen window, Coffee Percolator saw the three of them turning into the Dimbleby's gate next-door with his bright red eye.

'Quick!' Salt cried, hopping out of the soup

ladle in the silver drawer.

'Ready!' sneezed Pepper, skipping from behind an onion on the chopping board.

And Whizz! Whirr! Bang! Clang! Doors opened and shut. Lids jumped off and on. All the kitchen folk rattled their cords in excitement as Salt and Pepper answered their wishes and changed their jobs about. Mr Cherry's shirts rose from Washing Machine and flew over into Oven. Doughy unbaked plum tarts skimmed from Oven to Icebox. Coffee Percolator gulped down cold ice cream. Finally they were all set. Wouldn't Mrs Cherry be surprised when she came back! How she would praise their talent!

But what the kitchen folk didn't know was that they were going to be surprised themselves sooner than they thought. Mr Cherry's work finished earlier than he planned, and even now he was whistling home down Appleton Lane to surprise Mrs Cherry in time for lunch.

'Blrip! Blrip!' exclaimed Coffee Percolator, trying to keep the ice cream cold. But try as he would, the

ice cream melted and grew hotter and hotter, bubbling up under his lid and foaming out onto the table.

'Oh dearr, dearrr!' whirred Egg-Beater. 'I beat and beat, but Mrs Cherry's blouses only tie into knots with no frills at all. Look what knots I've got them into! Oh, dear!'

'Bump! Bump!' Iron hopped up and down on the ironing board, plunging his silver point into the waffle batter Mrs Cherry had mixed up for her lunch. 'Bump!' But the waffle batter only stood in a sticky puddle and every time Iron made a dent, the batter splattered onto his shiny face and all over the kitchen wall.

'Brumm! Brummm! Brummmm!'

Washing Machine's cake dough went whirling round and round in a soggy slush, no nearer to being an airy yellow sponge cake than it had been five minutes ago.

Toaster wept tears and steamed instead of popping out beautifully shaped icecubes.

'Oh dear! Oh dear!' the kitchen folk chorused. 'This is hard work! This is worse than we bargained for!'

From their ringside seat in the kitchen matchbox, Salt and Pepper exchanged knowing winks.

But then, right in the midst of these wails and groans, who should stalk into the kitchen but Mr Cherry, looking for his round, rosy-cheeked wife.

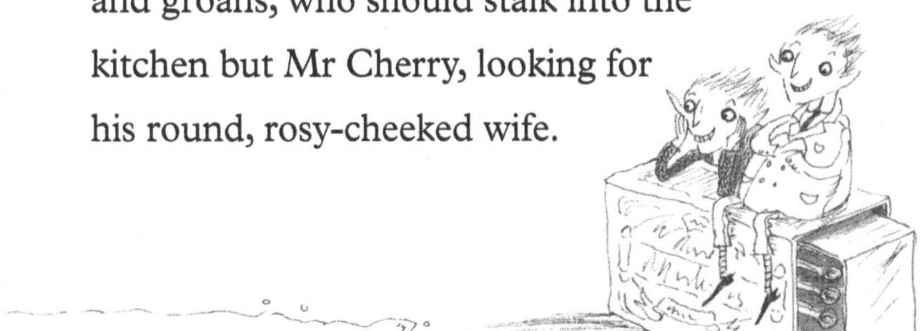

Mr Cherry blinked. Mr Cherry gaped. A smell of roasting shirts rose from the oven. The coffee percolator burbled and foamed strangely. Waffle batter polka-dotted the walls. Mr Cherry staggered to the icebox and opened the door for a quietening snack of cheese and pickles and found a dozen doughy frost-bitten plum tarts staring him in the face.

Salt and Pepper clutched each other in dismay, crouching down behind Mrs Cherry's sweet-scented box of cloves. What an expression on Mr Cherry's face! How would they ever clean up the terrible clutter the kitchen folk had made before Mrs Cherry came back?

'Myrtle! Myrtle!' Mr Cherry cried, running out onto the back porch waving his hands. At that same moment, Coffee Percolator's red eye spotted Mrs Cherry coming up the back walk with Sunny and Bunny.

'Quick!' coughed Coffee Percolator. 'Fill me up with my fragrant black coffee again!'

'Please,' begged Oven. 'Give me back my sponge cake. And my plum tarts. These shirts taste terrible!'

And from every corner Salt and Pepper heard the same cry: 'Oh, let me do my own work once again!'

Quicker than a wink and a blink, they jumped

to work. Whizz! Whirr! Bang! Clang! Doors opened and shut Lids jumped off and on. Cords rattled. Salt and Pepper huffed and puffed, and scrimbled and scrambled, and rubbed and scrubbed. And in the nick of time, too.

'J—just look!' Mr Cherry's trembling voice was saying outside the kitchen door. 'Just see what's happened to your kitchen, Myrtle!'

Mrs Cherry sailed into the kitchen, followed by Sunny and Bunny, each twin holding a tiny kitten. Sunny's kitten was all white, Bunny's all black. Mr Cherry came in last, spectacles in his hand, huffing on them and polishing them with his best pocket handkerchief. He seemed very upset.

'Why, what's the matter?' Mrs Cherry asked.

'Did you smell something burning?' Whisk! Mrs Cherry opened the oven door and took out a feathery gold sponge cake and a tray of hot plum tarts.

'Mmmm!' chorused the Dimbleby twins.

Mr Cherry was too surprised for words.

'Whoops!' Up came Washing Machine's lid. Mrs Cherry lifted out a pile of damp snow-white shirts to lay beside the frilly blouses Iron had finished. Click! Icebox produced a chunk of vanilla ice cream which Mrs Cherry ladled into two blue saucers, one for Sunny, one for Bunny, to celebrate Fudge Ripple's five new kittens.

'Waffles for lunch!' Mrs Cherry announced, lifting the top of Waffle-Iron to show two crisp brown waffly waffles.

'Mmm!' Mr Cherry said, blinking behind his spectacles. 'I must have been seeing things!'

When Sunny and Bunny had gone home, Sunny holding a hot plum tart and a white kitten, Bunny holding a hot plum tart and a black kitten, Mr and Mrs Cherry sat down to lunch.

'Yum,' Mr Cherry said when he got to the plum tart. 'What a fine lunch!'

'It is good,' admitted Mrs Cherry. 'Thanks to my oven.'

Salt and Pepper didn't say anything. They had fallen sound asleep side by side in the flour tin after Mrs Cherry's kitchen change-about and change-back-again!

The Bed Book

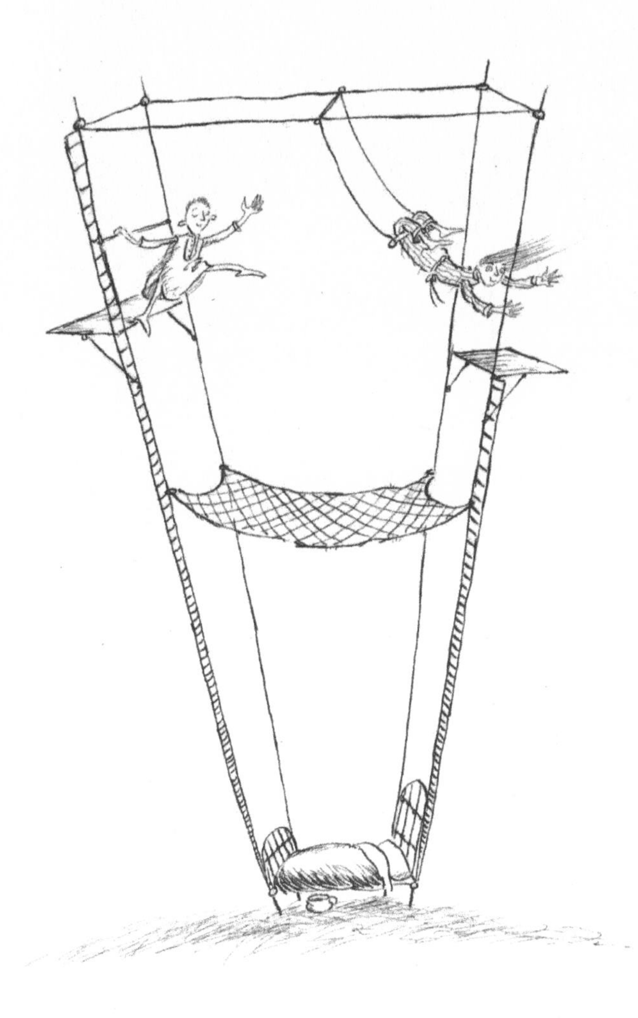

BEDS come in all sizes –
Single or double,
Cot-size or cradle,
King-size or trundle.

Most Beds are Beds
For sleeping or resting,
But the *best* Beds are much
More interesting!

Not just a white little
Tucked-in-tight little
Nighty-night little
Turn-out-the-light little Bed –

Instead
A Bed for Fishing,
A Bed for Cats,
A Bed for a Troupe of Acrobats.

The *right* sort of Bed
(If you see what I mean)
Is a Bed that might
Be a Submarine

Nosing through water
Clear and green,
Silver and glittery
As a sardine

Or a Jet-Propelled Bed
For visiting Mars
With mosquito nets
For the shooting stars.

If you get hungry
In the middle of the night
A Snack Bed is good
For the appetite –

With a pillow of bread
To nibble at
And up at the head
An automat

Where you need no shillings,
Just a finger to stick in
The slot, and out come
Cakes and cold chicken.

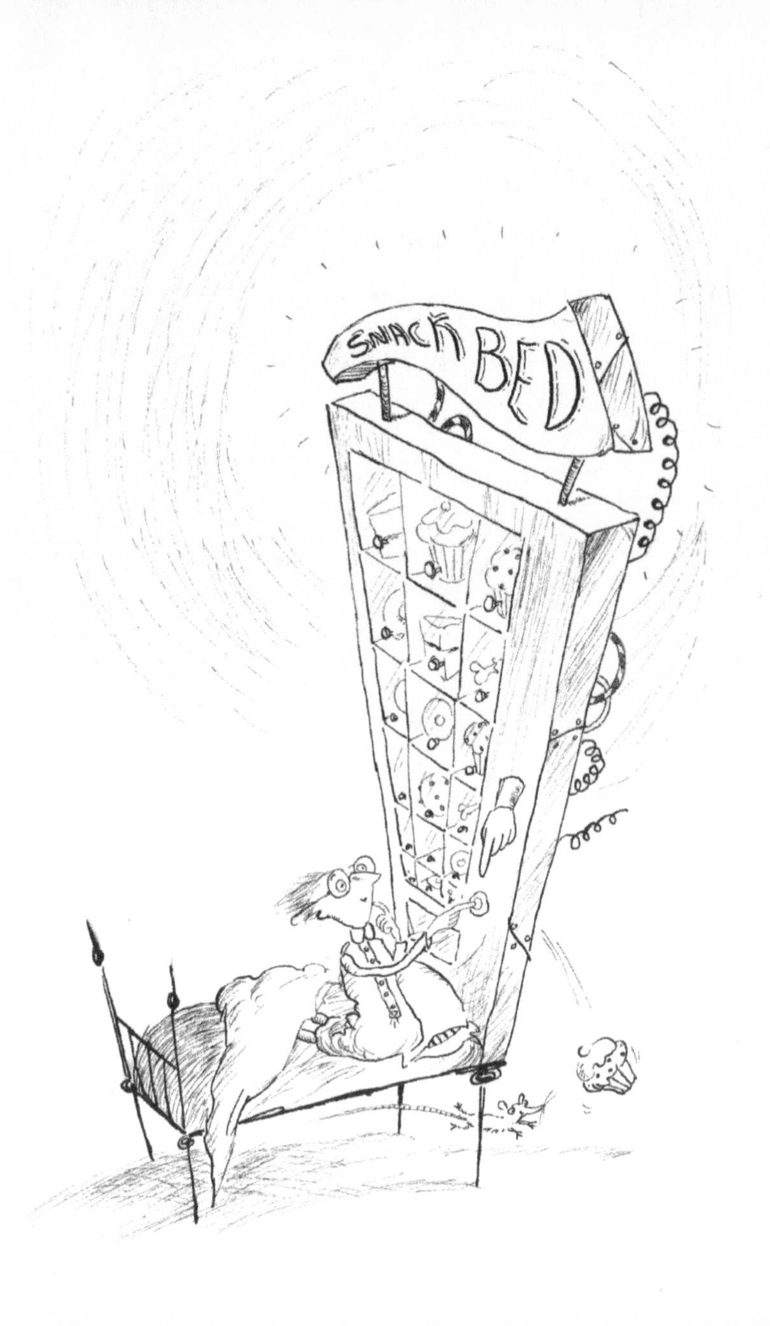
SNACK BED

Or if the dog and the cat
And the parakeet
Dance on the covers
With muddyish feet.

In a Spottable Bed
It *never* matters
Where jam rambles
And where paint splatters!

On the other hand,
If you want to *move*
A Tank Bed's the Bed
Most movers approve.

A Tank Bed's got cranks
And wheels and cogs
And levers to pull
If you're stuck in bogs.

A Tank Bed's treads
Go upstairs or down,
Through duck ponds or through
A cobbledy town.

And you're snug inside
If it rains or hails.
A Tank Bed's got
Everything but sails!

Now a gentler Bed
Is a good deal more
The sort of Bed
Bird-Watchers adore –

A kind of hammock
Between two tall trees
Where you can swing
In the leaves at ease

And count all the birds –
Wren, robin and rook –
And write their names
In a Naming Book.

Around Bird-Watching Beds
You hang nests of straw
For hummingbirds, hoopoes
And the great macaw.

All the birds would flock
(If I'm not mistaken)
To your berries and cherries
And bits of bacon.

None of these Beds,
Of course, is very
Easy to fold up
Or fetch and carry

So a Pocket-size Bed
Is a fine Bed to own.
When you're eating out
With friend Jim or Aunt Joan

And they say: *It's too bad*
You can't stay overnight
But there isn't an extra
Bed in sight

You can take out your Bed
Shrunk small as a pea
And water it till
It grows suitably.

Yes, a Pocket-size Bed
Works very well
Only how can you tell,
O how can you tell

It won't shrink back
To the size of a pea
While you're asleep in it?
Then where would you be!

O here is a Bed
Shrinkproofer than that,
A floatier, boatier
Bed than that!

In an Elephant Bed
You go where you please.
You pick bananas
Right out of the trees.

If the tigers jump up
When you happen to sneeze
Why, they can't jump higher
Than the elephant's knees.

An Elephant Bed
Is where kings ride.
It's cool as a pool
In the shade inside.

You can climb up the trunk
And slide down behind.
Everyone knows
Elephants don't mind! –

When it's even too hot
For the Hottentot
A trunk-spray shower's
There on the spot.

But when it's lots
Of degrees below,
A North-Pole Bed
Is the best I know.

It's warm as toast
Under ten feet of snow.
It's warm as the Bed
Of an Eskimo.

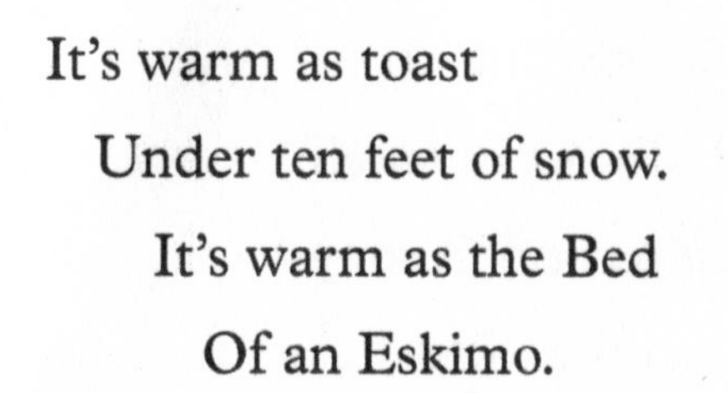

A North-Pole Bed
Is made of fur.
It's fine if you're
An ex-plor-er,

Or if you just
Have a very cold nose.
There's a built-in oven
To warm your toes.

O who cares much
If a Bed's big or small
Or lumpy and bumpy –
Who cares at all

As long as its springs
Are bouncy and new.
From a Bounceable Bed
You bounce into the blue –

Over the hollyhocks
(Toodle-oo!)
Over the owls'
To-whit-to-whoo,

Over the moon
To Timbuktoo
With springier springs
Than a kangaroo.

You can see if the Big Dipper's
Full of stew,
And you may want to stay
Up a week or two.

These are the Beds
For me and for you!
These are the Beds
To climb into: